JE

A LIFT-THE-FLAP BOOK

CORDUROY'S BIRTHDAY

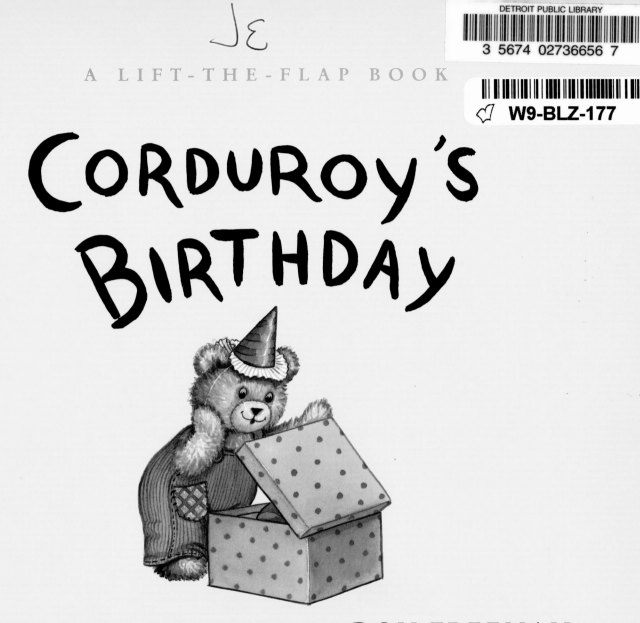

BASED ON THE CHARACTER BY DON FREEMAN
STORY BY B. G. HENNESSY
PICTURES BY LISA McCUE

VIKING

CH
R

Today is Corduroy's birthday! He is very excited.
After breakfast he checks his mailbox. There are three
birthday cards and a note. The note says that Corduroy
should come to Checkerboard Bunny's house at three o'clock.
Who tied those balloons to Corduroy's mailbox?

Corduroy wonders what he can do until three o'clock.
He decides to clean up. He recycles his newspapers
and donates clothes that no longer fit him to the children's
shelter. Corduroy has grown a lot this year!
He also chooses some cans of food for the food bank.

Corduroy's friends are busy, too. They are planning a surprise party for Corduroy. They are making a cake, some cards, and birthday decorations. *Sshhhhh*—don't tell Corduroy!

It's three o'clock!
Corduroy knocks on Checkerboard Bunny's door.
Where could Checkerboard Bunny be?
SURPRISE! HAPPY BIRTHDAY, CORDUROY!

Now it's time to play some games.
Who will break the piñata?
Isn't that clown funny?

Corduroy's friends have planned a treasure hunt.
Who will find the most treasure?

Finally it's time for the birthday cake.
Corduroy makes a wish before he blows out the candles.
Happy Birthday, Corduroy!

DON FREEMAN was born in San Diego, California, and moved to New York City to study art, making his living as a jazz trumpeter. Following the loss of his trumpet on a subway train, Mr. Freeman turned his talents to art full-time. In the 1940s, he began writing and illustrating children's books. His many popular titles include *Corduroy*, *A Pocket for Corduroy*, *Beady Bear*, *Dandelion*, *Mop Top*, and *Norman the Doorman*.

LISA McCUE was born in Tappan, New York, and has illustrated more than seventy-five books, including *Corduroy's Halloween*, *Corduroy's Christmas*, *Corduroy's Toys*, *Corduroy's Day* and *Corduroy on the Go*. She lives in Bethlehem, Pennsylvania, with her husband and their two sons.

VIKING
Published by the Penguin Group
Penguin Books USA Inc., 375 Hudson Street, New York, New York 10014, U.S.A.
Penguin Books Ltd, 27 Wrights Lane, London W8 5TZ, England
Penguin Books Australia Ltd, Ringwood, Victoria, Australia
Penguin Books Canada Ltd, 10 Alcorn Avenue, Toronto, Ontario, Canada M4V 3B2
Penguin Books (N.Z.) Ltd, 182-190 Wairau Road, Auckland 10, New Zealand

Penguin Books Ltd, Registered Offices: Harmondsworth, Middlesex, England

First published in 1997 by Viking, a division of Penguin Books USA Inc.

1   3   5   7   9   10   8   6   4   2

Text copyright © Penguin Books USA Inc., 1997
Illustrations copyright © Lisa McCue, 1997
All rights reserved

ISBN 0-670-87065-X

Printed in Singapore   Set in Stempel Garamond